Rudyard KIPLING

The Elephant's Child

illustrated by Arlette Lavie

Published by Child's Play (International) Ltd
Swindon   **Bologna**   **New York**
© M. Twinn 1986   ISBN 0-85953-275-5   Printed in Singapore
This impression 1991   Library of Congress Catalogue Number 90-46609

IN the High and Far-Off Times
the Elephant, O Best Beloved,
had no trunk. He had only
a blackish, bulgy nose,
as big as a boot, that he could
wriggle about from side to side;
but he couldn't pick up
things with it. But there was
one Elephant—a new Elephant—
an Elephant's Child—who was
full of 'satiable curtiosity,
and that means he asked
ever so many questions.
And he lived in Africa,
and he filled all Africa
with his 'satiable curtiosities.

He asked his tall aunt, the Ostrich,
why her tail-feathers grew just so,
and his tall aunt the Ostrich spanked him
with her hard, hard claw.

He asked
his tall uncle,
the Giraffe, what
made his skin spotty,
and his tall uncle,
the Giraffe,
spanked him
with his hard,
hard hoof.
And still he was
full of 'satiable
curtiosity!

He asked his broad aunt, the Hippopotamus,
why her eyes were red, and his broad aunt, the Hippopotamus,
spanked him with her broad, broad hoof.

And he asked his hairy uncle, the Baboon,
why melons tasted just so, and his hairy uncle,
the Baboon, spanked him with his hairy, hairy paw.
And *still* he was full of 'satiable curtiosity!

He asked questions about everything
that he saw, or heard, or felt, or smelt,
or touched, and all his uncles
and his aunts spanked him.
And still he was full
of 'satiable curtiosity!

One fine morning in the middle
of the Precession of the Equinoxes
this 'satiable Elephant's Child
asked a new fine question
that he had never asked before.
He asked, 'What does the Crocodile
have for dinner?'
Then everybody said, 'Hush!'
in a loud and dretful tone,
and they spanked him
immediately and directly,
without stopping,
for a long time.

By and by, when that was finished,
he came upon Kolokolo Bird
sitting in the middle of a wait-a-bit
thorn-bush, and he said,
'My father has spanked me,
and my mother has spanked me;
all my aunts and uncles have spanked me
for my 'satiable curtiosity; and *still*
I want to know what the Crocodile has for dinner!'
    Then Kolokolo Bird said, with a mournful cry,
'Go to the banks of the great grey-green, greasy
Limpopo River, all set about with fever-trees, and find out.'

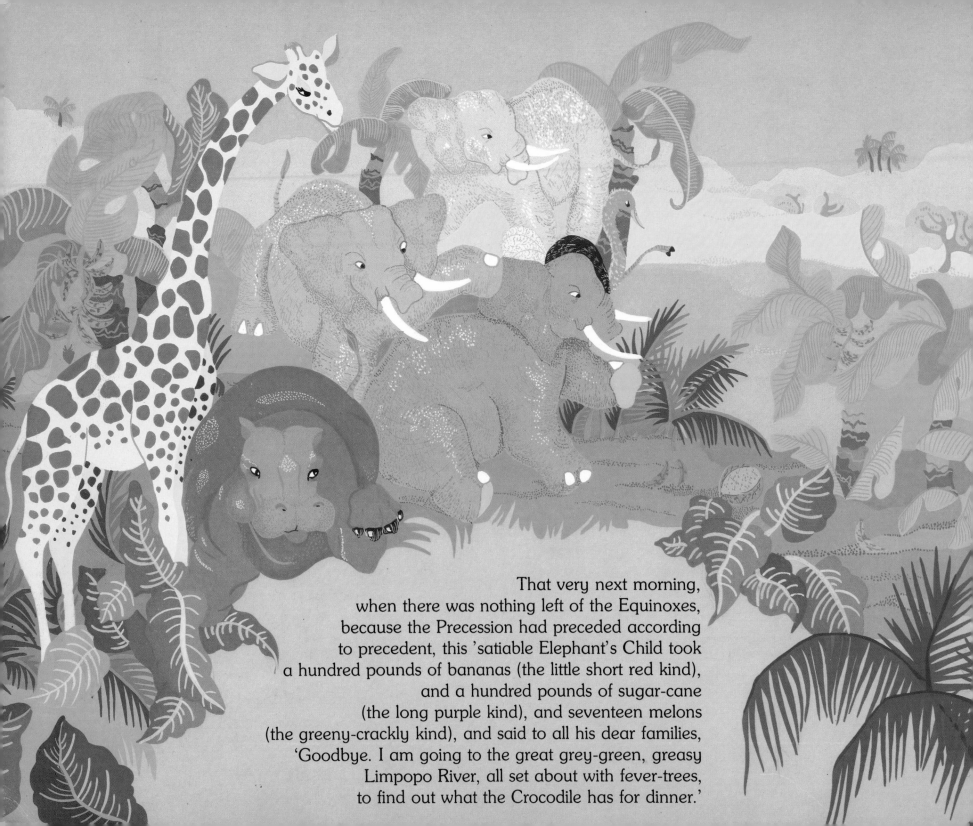

That very next morning,
when there was nothing left of the Equinoxes,
because the Precession had preceded according
to precedent, this 'satiable Elephant's Child took
a hundred pounds of bananas (the little short red kind),
and a hundred pounds of sugar-cane
(the long purple kind), and seventeen melons
(the greeny-crackly kind), and said to all his dear families,
'Goodbye. I am going to the great grey-green, greasy
Limpopo River, all set about with fever-trees,
to find out what the Crocodile has for dinner.'

And they all spanked him once more for luck,
though he asked them most politely to stop.

Then he went away, a little warm,
but not at all astonished,
eating melons, and throwing the rind about,
because he could not pick it up.

He went from Graham's Town to Kimberley,
and from Kimberley to Khama's Country,
and from Khama's Country he went east by north,
eating melons all the time, till at last he came to the banks
of the great grey-green, greasy Limpopo River,
all set about with fever-trees,
precisely as Kolokolo Bird had said.

Now you must know and understand, O Best Beloved,
that till that very week, and day, and hour, and minute,
this 'satiable Elephant's Child had never seen a Crocodile,
and did not know what one was like. It was all his 'satiable curtiosity.

The first thing that he found
was a Bi-Coloured-Python-Rock-Snake curled round a rock.

''Scuse me,' said the Elephant's Child
most politely, 'but have you seen such a thing
as a Crocodile in these promiscuous parts?'
'*Have* I seen a Crocodile?'
said the Bi-Coloured-Python-Rock-Snake,
in a voice of dretful scorn.
'What will you ask me next?'

''Scuse me,' said the Elephant's Child,
'but could you kindly tell me
what he has for dinner?'

Then the Bi-Coloured-Python-Rock-Snake
uncoiled himself very quickly from the rock,
and spanked the Elephant's Child
with his scalesome, flailsome tail.

'That is odd,' said the Elephant's Child,
'because my father and my mother,
and my uncle and my aunt, not to mention
my other aunt, the Hippopotamus,
and my other uncle, the Baboon,
have all spanked me for my 'satiable curtiosity
—and I suppose this is the same thing.'

So he said good-bye very politely
to the Bi-Coloured-Python-Rock-Snake,
and helped to coil him up on the rock again,
and went on, a little warm, but not at all astonished,
eating melons, and throwing the rind about,
because he could not pick it up,
till he trod on what he thought
was a log of wood at the very edge
of the great grey-green, greasy Limpopo River,
all set about with fever-trees.

But it was really the Crocodile, O Best Beloved,
and the Crocodile winked one eye—like this!

'Scuse me,' said the Elephant's Child most politely, 'but do you
happen to have seen a Crocodile
in these promiscuous parts?'

Then the Crocodile winked the other eye, and lifted
half his tail out of the mud; and the Elephant's Child stepped back
most politely, because he did not wish to be spanked again.

'Come hither, Little One,' said the Crocodile.
'Why do you ask such things?'

'Scuse me,' said the Elephant's Child most politely, 'but my father
has spanked me, my mother has spanked me, not to mention my tall aunt,
the Ostrich, and my tall uncle, the Giraffe, who can kick ever so hard,
as well as my broad aunt, the Hippopotamus, and my hairy uncle,
the Baboon, *and* including the Bi-Coloured-Python-Rock-Snake,
with the scalesome, flailsome tail, just up the bank,
who spanks harder than any of them; and *so*,
if it's quite all the same to you, I don't
want to be spanked any more.'

'Come hither, Little One,' said the Crocodile, 'for I am the Crocodile,' and he wept crocodile-tears to show it was quite true.

Then the Elephant's Child grew all breathless, and panted, and kneeled down on the bank and said, 'You are the very person I have been looking for all these long days. Will you please tell me what you have for dinner?'

'Come hither, Little One,' said the Crocodile, 'and I'll whisper.'

Then the Elephant's Child put his head down
close to the Crocodile's musky, tusky mouth,
and the Crocodile caught him by his little nose,
which up to that very week, day, hour, and minute,
had been no bigger than a boot, though much more useful.

'I think,' said the Crocodile—and he said it between his teeth, like this—
'I think to-day I will begin with Elephant's Child!'

At this, O Best Beloved, the Elephant's Child was much annoyed,
and he said, speaking through his nose, like this,
'Led go! You are hurtig be!'

Then the Bi-Coloured-Python-Rock-Snake scuffled down from the bank and said, 'My young friend, if you do not now, immediately and instantly, pull as hard as ever you can, it is my opinion that your acquaintance in the large-pattern leather ulster' (and by this he meant the Crocodile) 'will jerk you into yonder limpid stream before you can say Jack Robinson.'

This is the way Bi-Coloured-Python-Rock-Snakes always talk.

Then the Elephant's Child
sat back on his little haunches,
and pulled, and pulled, and pulled,
and his nose began to stretch.
And the Crocodile floundered into the water,
making it all creamy with great sweeps
of his tail, and *he* pulled,
and pulled, and pulled.

And the Elephant's Child's nose
kept on stretching;
and the Elephant's Child
spread all his little four legs
and pulled, and pulled, and pulled,
and his nose kept on stretching;
and the Crocodile threshed his tail
like an oar, and *he* pulled,
and pulled, and pulled, and at each pull
the Elephant's Child's nose
grew longer and longer
—and it hurt him hijjus!

Then the Elephant's Child felt his legs slipping,
and he said through his nose, which was now
nearly five feet long, 'This is too butch for be!'

Then the Bi-Coloured-Python-Rock-Snake
came down from the bank,
and knotted himself in a double-clove-hitch
round the Elephant's Child's hind-legs, and said,
'Rash and inexperienced traveller, we will now
seriously devote ourselves to a little high tension,
because if we do not, it is my impression
that yonder self-propelling man-of-war
with the armour-plated upper deck'
(and by this, O Best Beloved, he meant the Crocodile)
'will permanently vitiate your future career.'
     That is the way all Bi-Coloured-Python-Rock-Snakes
always talk.
     So he pulled, and the Elephant's Child pulled,
and the Crocodile pulled . . .

. . . but the Elephant's Child and the Bi-Coloured-Python-Rock-Snake
pulled hardest; and at last the Crocodile let go
of the Elephant's Child's nose with a plop
that you could hear all up and down the Limpopo.

Then the Elephant's Child sat down
most hard and sudden;
but first he was careful to say 'Thank you'
to the Bi-Coloured-Python-Rock-Snake;
and next he was kind to his poor pulled nose,
and wrapped it all up in cool banana leaves,
and hung it in the great grey-green,
greasy Limpopo to cool.

'What are you doing that for?'
said the Bi-Coloured-Python-Rock-Snake.

''Scuse me,' said the Elephant's Child,
'but my nose is badly out of shape,
and I am waiting for it to shrink.'

'Then you will have to wait a long time,'
said the Bi-Coloured-Python-Rock-Snake.
'Some people do not know what is good for them.'

The Elephant's Child sat there for three days
waiting for his nose to shrink. But it never
grew any shorter, and, besides, it made him squint.
For, O Best Beloved, you will see
and understand that the Crocodile
had pulled it out into a really truly trunk
same as all Elephants have to-day.

At the end of the third day a fly came
and stung him on the shoulder,
and before he knew what he was doing
he lifted up his trunk and hit that fly dead with the end of it.
"Vantage number one!" said the Bi-Coloured-Python-Rock-Snake.
'You couldn't have done that with a mere-smear nose.
Try and eat a little now.'

Before he thought what he was doing
the Elephant's Child put out his trunk
and plucked a large bundle of grass,
dusted it clean against his fore-legs,
and stuffed it into his own mouth.

''Vantage number two!'
said the Bi-Coloured-Python-Rock-Snake.
'You couldn't have done that with a mere-smear nose.
Don't you think the sun is very hot here?'

'It is,' said the Elephant's Child, and before he thought what he was doing he schlooped up a schloop of mud from the banks of the great grey-green, greasy Limpopo, and slapped it on his head where it made a cool schloopy-sloshy mud-cap all trickly behind his ears.

''Vantage number three!' said the Bi-Coloured-Python-Rock-Snake. 'You couldn't have done that with a mere-smear nose. Now how do you feel about being spanked again?'

''Scuse me,' said the Elephant's Child,
'but I should not like it at all.'

'How would you like to spank somebody?'
said the Bi-Coloured-Python-Rock-Snake.

'I should like it very much indeed,'
said the Elephant's Child.

'Well,' said the Bi-Coloured-Python-Rock-Snake,
'you will find that new nose of yours
very useful to spank people with.'

'Thank you,' said the Elephant's Child,
'I'll remember that; and now I think
I'll go home to all my dear families and try.'

So the Elephant's Child went home across Africa frisking and whisking his trunk. When he wanted fruit to eat he pulled fruit down from a tree, instead of waiting for it to fall as he used to do. When he wanted grass he plucked grass up from the ground, instead of going on his knees as he used to do. When the flies bit him he broke off the branch of a tree and used it as a fly-whisk; and he made himself a new, cool, slushy-squshy mud-cap whenever the sun was hot. When he felt lonely walking through Africa he sang to himself down his trunk, and the noise was louder than several brass bands.

He went specially out of his way to find a broad Hippopotamus
(she was no relation of his), and he spanked her very hard,
to make sure that the Bi-Coloured-Python-Rock-Snake
had spoken the truth about his new trunk.
The rest of the time he picked up the melon-rings
that he had dropped on his way to the Limpopo—
for he was a Tidy Pachyderm.

One dark evening he came back to all his dear families,
and he coiled up his trunk and said, 'How do you do?'
They were very glad to see him, and immediately said,
'Come here and be spanked for your 'satiable curtiosity.'
   'Pooh,' said the Elephant's Child. 'I don't think you peoples know
anything about spanking; but *I* do, and I'll show you.'
   Then he uncurled his trunk and knocked
two of his dear brothers head over heels.
'O Bananas!' said they, 'where did you learn
that trick, and what have you done to your nose?'

'I got a new one from the Crocodile on the banks
of the great grey-green, greasy Limpopo River,'
said the Elephant's Child. 'I asked him what he had
for dinner, and he gave me this to keep.'

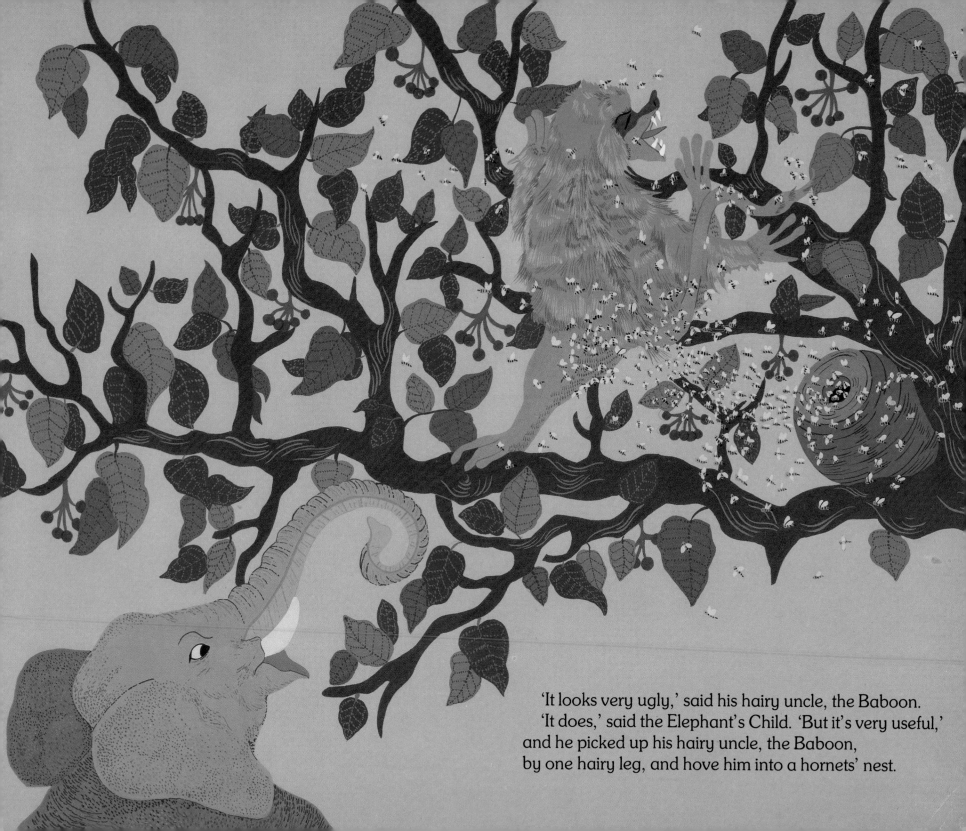

'It looks very ugly,' said his hairy uncle, the Baboon.
'It does,' said the Elephant's Child. 'But it's very useful,'
and he picked up his hairy uncle, the Baboon,
by one hairy leg, and hove him into a hornets' nest.

Then that bad Elephant's Child spanked all his dear families for a long time, till they were very warm and greatly astonished. He pulled out his tall Ostrich aunt's tail-feathers; and he caught his tall uncle, the Giraffe, by the hind-leg, and dragged him through a thorn-bush; and he shouted at his broad aunt, the Hippopotamus, and blew bubbles into her ear when she was sleeping in the water after meals; but he never let any one touch Kolokolo Bird.

At last things grew so exciting that his dear families
went off one by one in a hurry to the banks
of the great grey-green, greasy Limpopo River,
all set about with fever-trees,
to borrow new noses from the Crocodile.

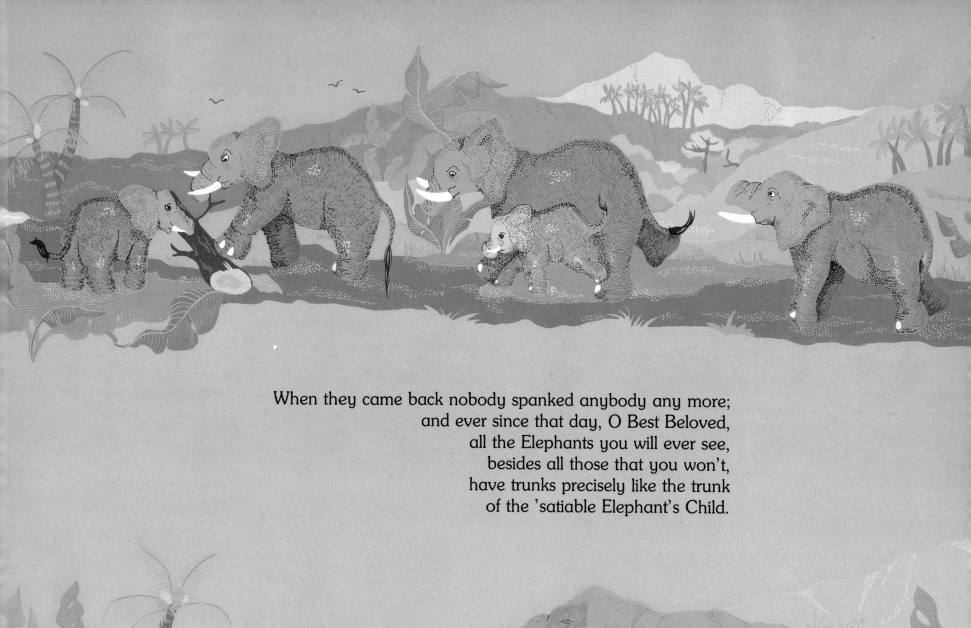

When they came back nobody spanked anybody any more;
and ever since that day, O Best Beloved,
all the Elephants you will ever see,
besides all those that you won't,
have trunks precisely like the trunk
of the 'satiable Elephant's Child.